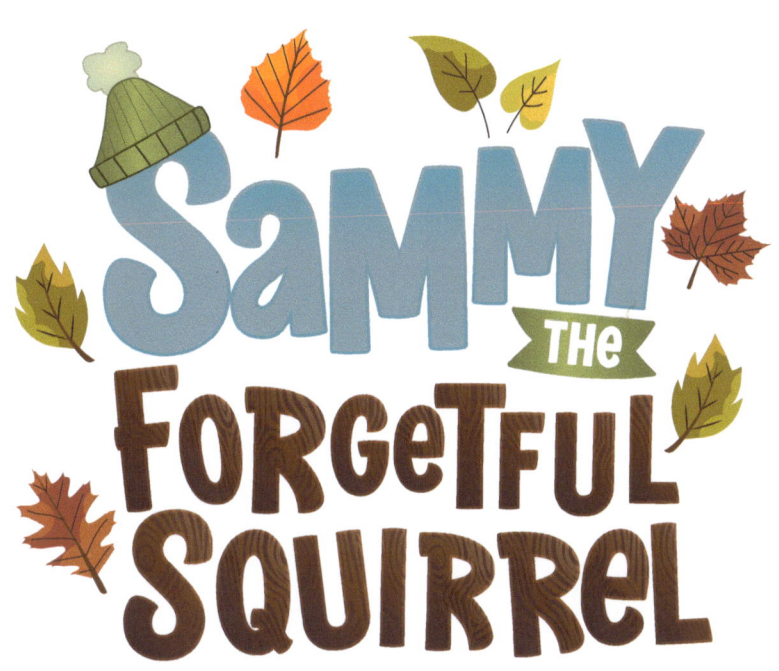

To Alun, my wonderful husband who looks after all the animals and wildlife who visit our garden.

The support from my family, Alison and Danny.

Friends who tirelessly rescue animals, Fay, Sybil and Karl.

My loyal friend Sue who has been by my side throughout my life.

Finally, all the wonderful staff at Bear With Us Productions especially Andy, for the support and encouragement in bringing this book to life.

Published in association with Bear With Us Productions

Illustration by Johanna Zverzina
Graphic design by Katie Owens

www.justbearwithus.com

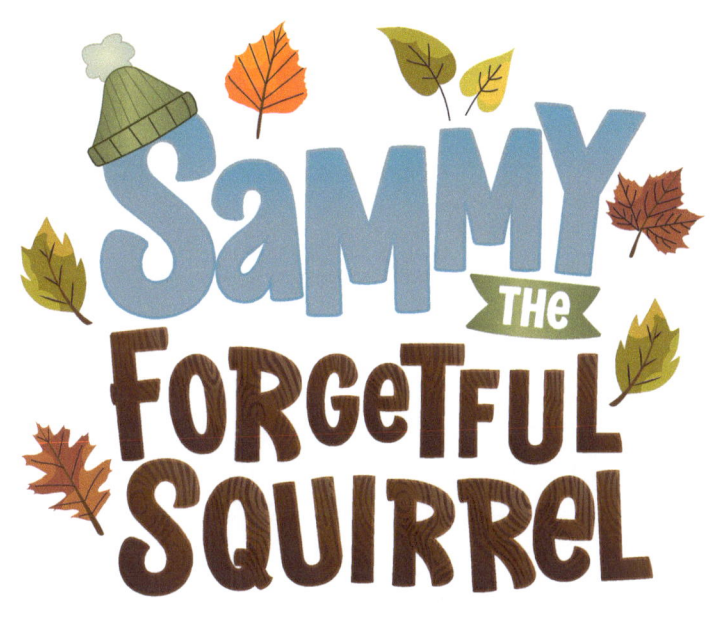

Sammy the Forgetful Squirrel

Written by Caroline Jones

Illustrated By Johanna Zverzina

BEAR WITH US PRODUCTIONS

Sammy the Squirrel wakes up in his bed.
Feeling cold he pulls the covers over his head,
Then stretches his arms and wiggles his toes.

Sammy is still cold so gets up and puts
on more clothes:

A green hat, a blue coat and small red boots too.
Winter is coming and Sammy knows what to do!

For many months Sammy has buried lots of nuts.
His tummy rumbles as he imagines digging them up.

Sammy's family and friends depend on him
To feed them when the cold winter comes in.

The nuts he has buried will fill them all,
Because he collected so many this Fall.

Whether the animals in the forest are **big** or small
Every winter Sammy has a party, inviting them all.
They all get excited, from young to old,
As Sammy puts a sign up, which is **big and bold.**

Sammy walks through the forest, snowflakes falling around.
He is worried and shudders; will the nuts still be found?

"If the snow falls thick and fast,
How will I know where I saw the nuts last?"
He can't make up his mind as he looks all around.
"Are they this way or that way? They've got to be found!"

The snow still falling, Sammy rushes from tree to tree,
Searching under bushes. "Where can the nuts be?"

He bends to tie his laces and pulls up his socks,
And jumps as he comes face to face with a fox!

"What's wrong, Sammy?" the fox asks, looking down
At the little squirrel whose face is wearing a frown.

"Winter is coming and I buried nuts to eat when it's cold,
The other squirrels need them today – young and old.
As well as to serve for our big party tonight.

Oh dear, oh dear, it has got to go right!"

"Don't worry, I'll help find them, the party will go ahead.
We'll fill our tums, sing and dance before it's time for bed."

They find no nuts despite the two looking desperately.
But there's something making a noise near a bush by a tree.

Suddenly, out from the bushes comes Billy, a **large boisterous badger**.
Sammy tells him about his plight and the nuts he is after.

Fox shouts with excitement and dances with glee.
"We are no longer alone, our two is now **three!**

Billy, you have such a **big** snout
That can help us sniff the nuts out!"

The three begin looking in both forest and park,
They must find the nuts before it gets dark.

The snow stops falling and it starts to rain,
But the three still plod on, searching in vain.

They grow tired with each step that they take,
But they carry on even though their paws ache.

They hear a noise up high in a tree.
The three look up and see it's Owlie.

Now Sammy has heard that owls are wise,
And as he begins wiping rain from his eyes,

He hears Owlie ask: "Whatever is wrong?"

"I've lost the nuts, and we've searched for so long!"

The owl thinks for a moment then flies down from the tree.
And soon he is standing in front of the three.
As Owlie speaks everyone begins to listen,
Whilst snow on the branches shimmer and glisten.

"We are your friends and will help you find the nuts.
Think back to when you hid them and recall the steps that you took."

Sammy thinks hard. "I left my home with nuts galore,
As I had gathered so many, much more than before!"

"Where you went may become clear,
If we take a walk around and look at what's near."

They cannot find the nuts and wonder what to do.

The animals want to help Sammy, concern on their faces.

The four walk deeper into the forest, looking in different places.

Will they find them before the night is through?

Sammy makes them jump as he shouts out with glee:

"I remember! I buried them here by this tree!
It's the **biggest tree** that I've ever met,
I thought if I buried them here, I'd never forget!"

The four uncover the nuts as the forest grows dark,
And carry them carefully home through the park.

The friends help Sammy put the party sign on his door.
Soon animals begin to arrive by the score.

Welcome to Rumbletums! nuts are here!!

The notice reads the same as it does every year:

WELCOME TO RUMBLETUMS – NUTS ARE HERE!

At Sammy's party there are nuts for you all,
Whether young or old, or big or small.

By the fire the animals sing and dance,
And they watch in amazement as reindeer prance.
When every animal can fill their tummies no more,
They begin making their sleepy ways to the door.

They are happy and smiley because they've been fed,
And can return home to their warm comfy beds.

For his new friends, Sammy is glad,
They turned the day around to good from bad.
Sammy and friends will now have full tums,
And be warm and snug now the cold winter has come.

One thing that Sammy will never forget
Are the friends in the forest he has luckily met.

He thinks about next year's party as he closes his eyes.
Will you come along too and enjoy the surprise?

Caroline Jones

Caroline Jones lives in Wales with her husband Alun.
She qualified as a Drama and PE teacher and in 2010 achieved a BSc in
Complementary Therapy and Counselling.

For many years Caroline and Alun have rescued dogs and cats who need a home,
and proudly feed the animals and wildlife who visit the garden daily.

Caroline says "We are blessed to live in a former Forestry Commission house with forest all around us. The wildlife and animals are magical and inspiring.

Our friends visit and bring their children and grandchildren to see the wildlife and many times complete strangers out walking have stopped to chat and end up with a glass of squash and a seat on the patio. Life is far more fun if you share and why would we want to keep all of this for ourselves? It is enchanting.

Our garden has inspired me to write a children's book which I hope will be enjoyed and will stimulate a child's imagination. I hope to write many more about the animals and their unique characters.

Thank you for reading and maybe, if you are out walking, we will meet someday.

Cheerio for now,
Caroline

www.ingramcontent.com/pod-product-compliance
Lightning Source LLC
Chambersburg PA
CBHW041606120626
46551CB00002B/329